GLO GOES SHO

by Cheryl Willis Hudson
illustrated by Cathy Johnson

AFRO-BETS® is a registered trademark of Just Us Books.

The AFRO-BETS® characters were created by Wade and Cheryl Hudson.

Inquiries should be addressed to

JUST US BOOKS, INC.

356 Glenwood Ave. East Orange, NJ 07017

Printed in Mexico First Edition

10 9 8 7 6 5 4 3 2 1

Library of Congress Cataloging in Publication Data is available.

ISBN: 0-940975-84-X

Today is Nandi's
birthday and
Glo is going
shopping for a
special gift for
her friend.

All night long
Glo has been
dreaming about
the wonderful
things she
can buy.

Glo bounces out of bed.

She washes up, brushes
her teeth and gets
dressed.

Glo is ready to go and
she knows her mother
is ready, too.

"Let's see..." Glo's mind is racing as she and her mother enter the mall.

She rushes ahead of her mother.

"There are so many stores here!" beams Glo. "I'm sure I will find a gift that is just perfect for Nandi."

"I won't stop here," Glo says, walking quickly past the grocery store.

"But I bet this is where Nandi's mother will shop for the birthday cake and party favors."

Something bright catches Glo's eye at a store nearby.

"This jewelry is gorgeous! I love it!"

Then Glo thinks for a minute. "But this stuff is not quite right for Nandi. She doesn't like bright and shiny things like I do."

"What about some alligator go-go boots?" Glo giggles as she skips up to the shoe store window.

She goes inside and tries them on.

"Oh, no!" laughs Glo. "My friend, Nandi, is definitely not the go-go type."

At her next stop, Glo spots
some skates.

They look like fun!

Would Nandi like to try them?
Glo wonders.

Then Glo follows the sounds coming from the store next door.

She sees a radio with earphones.

Maybe she and Nandi could listen to their favorite music together.

Glo takes a deep breath in the plant shop, then looks at her mother who has been watching patiently.

"What about a special plant for my friend?" she asks.

"This red one here would brighten up Nandi's room."

Glo's mom just smiles.

They walk a little farther.

"Nandi likes to go places and explore new things," Glo says out loud.

"Maybe she'd like something from this store."

Glo reaches up and gives the globe a gentle spin.

"Look, Mommy!" shouts Glo.

"Gerbils, gold fish, guppies, golden canaries and German shepherd puppies!"

"This shop has lots of cute animals but would Nandi's mother let her keep a pet?"

"Ahhhh!" says Glo, running into her favorite boutique.

"...lacy gloves,
 ...lovely ribbons,
 ...a glittering party dress,
 ...dainty golden purses,
 ...glamorous sun glasses
    with rhinestone rims!"

Glo just can't resist buying something for herself.

The Food Court is just ahead. *I need to take a break*, Glo thinks to herself.

So she stops at the sweet shop for cookies and frozen yogurt.

"Yummy!"

But now it's getting late and there's only one store left. Will Glo ever find a gift for Nandi?

Glo thinks about Nandi and the things she likes to do.

What would her friend really like? For Nandi, a gift must be practical *and* fun.

Suddenly, Glo knows what to get. She runs down the aisle, pays for two items, gets them wrapped and hurries to Nandi's house.

TOYS, BOOKS & GAMES

Glo has found the perfect thing for her good friend, indeed.

What a double treat!

GLO GOES SHOPPING
by Cheryl Willis Hudson
illustrated by Cathy Johnson

Cheryl Willis Hudson is the author of several books for children, including *AFRO-BETS*® *A B C Book; Good Morning, Baby; Many Colors of Mother Goose;* and *Bright Eyes, Brown Skin* (co-authored with Bernette Ford). She is also co-founder with her husband, Wade, of Just Us Books, Inc.

Cathy Johnson is an accomplished illustrator-graphic designer. She has illustrated several books for children, including *Many Colors of Mother Goose* and *Robo's Favorite Places*. Johnson lives in Kansas City, Missouri, where she operates the graphic design studio, LUV-IT.

****

For Joanne, Frances and Marcia, my sister-friends. Happy shopping!

CH

For my wonderful nieces: Briana, Amber, Kierra and Traci.

Love, Auntie (CJ)